THE WISE MAN AND THE PROPHET MUSA عليه السلام

Quran Stories for Little Hearts

by

SANIYASNAIN KHAN

Goodwordkidz

Helping you build a family of faith

During the long journey to the Promised Land, the Prophet Musa عليه السلام learned many lessons. One of these was from al-Khidr ("the green one"). Probably an angel in the form of a man, al-Khidr had special knowledge and the power to make great changes in the affairs of the world.

The Prophet Musa عليه السلام began his long and tiring journey along the seashore, making a vow to reach this special servant of Allah: "I will not stop searching until I find the place where the two seas meet."

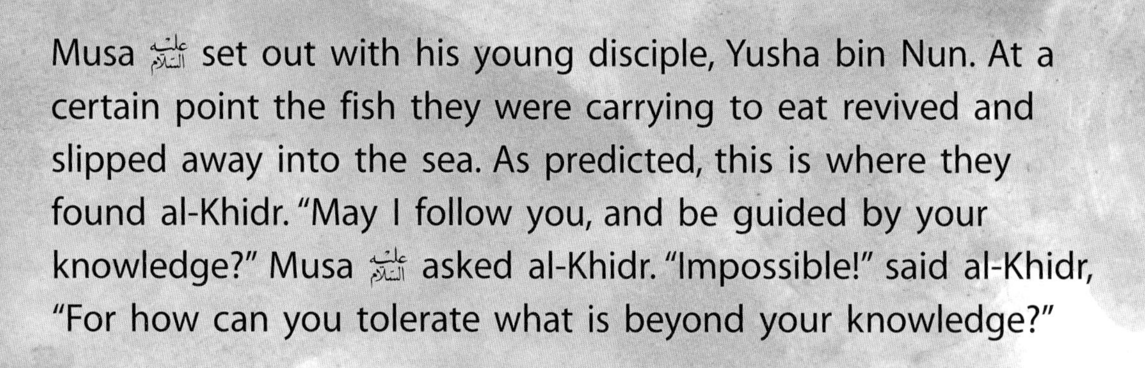

Musa عليه السلام set out with his young disciple, Yusha bin Nun. At a certain point the fish they were carrying to eat revived and slipped away into the sea. As predicted, this is where they found al-Khidr. "May I follow you, and be guided by your knowledge?" Musa عليه السلام asked al-Khidr. "Impossible!" said al-Khidr, "For how can you tolerate what is beyond your knowledge?"

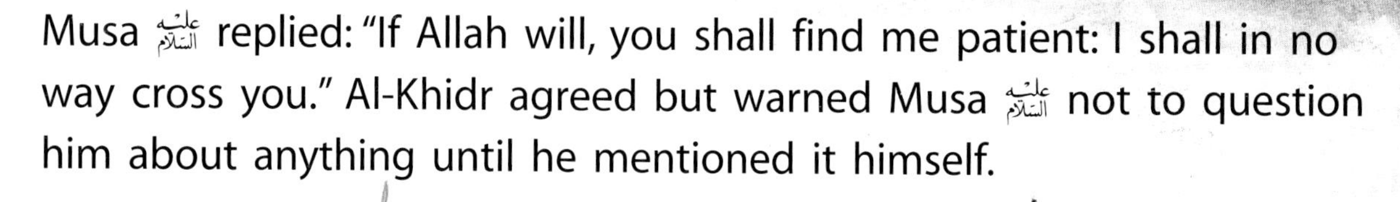

Musa عليه السلام replied: "If Allah will, you shall find me patient: I shall in no way cross you." Al-Khidr agreed but warned Musa عليه السلام not to question him about anything until he mentioned it himself.

The two then embarked upon a ship, whereupon al-Khidr bored a hole in it. Musa عليه السلام exclaimed: "Do you want to drown the passengers?" "Didn't I tell you," replied al-Khidr, "that you would not bear with me?" "Forgive me," said Musa عليه السلام. "Please don't be angry."

They journeyed on until they met a young boy, whom al-Khidr promptly killed. Musa عليه السلام exclaimed: "What wickedness—killing an innocent soul!"

"Didn't I tell you," al-Khidr replied, "that you would not bear with me?" Musa عليه السلام said: "If ever I question you again, abandon me; for then I should deserve it."

Then they came to a city and asked for food, but were refused. Seeing a wall that was crumbling, al-Khidr repaired it, but Musa عليه السلام objected to his doing so without payment.

"Now we must part," said al-Khidr. "But first I will explain my actions which seemed so dreadful to you. I damaged the ship because it belonged to some poor fishermen and nearby there was a king who plundered every vessel."

"As for the youth, he would only have distressed his believing parents with his wickedness and unbelief. We prayed that their Lord would replace him with a more righteous and filial son.

"The wall belonged to two orphans, sons of an honest man in the city. Beneath it their treasure lay buried. Your Lord decreed that they should dig it up when they grew to manhood. What I did was not by my will. That explains what you could not bear to watch with patience."

All this shows that the highest Divine wisdom sometimes appears to bring calamity. Man's limited knowledge and lack of foresight cause him to grieve over seeming tragedies. But the true believer never flinches at such times, for he knows that the loving hand of Allah unceasingly directs humanity toward the goal of the greatest good. This is the lesson of the story of al-Khidr.

Find Out More

To know more about the message and meaning of Allah's words, look up the following parts of the Quran which tell the story of the Prophet Musa عليه السلام and al-Khidr.

Surah al-Kahf 18:60-82

عليه السلام *Alayhis Salam* 'May peace be upon him.'
The customary blessings on the prophets.